APR 2014

S0-ADJ-238

City Homes

Heinemann
LIBRARY
Chicago, Illinois

© 2014 Heinemann Library
an imprint of Capstone Global Library, LLC
Chicago, Illinois

To contact Capstone Global Library please phone
800-747-4992, or visit our website www.capstonepub.com

All rights reserved. No part of this publication may be
reproduced or transmitted in any form or by any means,
electronic or mechanical, including photocopying, recording,
taping, or any information storage and retrieval system,
without permission in writing from the publisher.

Edited by Daniel Nunn and Abby Colich
Designed by Cynthia Akiyoshi
Picture research by Mica Brancic
Production by Sophia Argyris
Originated by Capstone Global Library
Printed and bound in China at RR Donnelly Asia Printing
Solutions

ISBN 978-1-4329-8065-8 (hc)
978-1-4329-8070-2 (pb)
17 16 15 14 13
10 9 8 7 6 5 4 3 2 1

Library of Congress Cataloging-in-Publication Data
Smith, Sian.
  City homes/ Sian Smith.
     pages cm.—(Where we live)
  Includes bibliographical references and index.
   ISBN 978-1-4329-8065-8 (hb)—ISBN 978-1-4329-8070-2
(pb) 1. Dwellings—Juvenile literature. 2. City dwellers—
Juvenile literature.
I. Title.

GT172.S656 2014
392.3'6—dc23   2012046416

Acknowledgments
We would like to thank the following for permission to
reproduce photographs: Getty Images pp. 4 (Cultura/Monty
Rakusen), 7 (The Image Bank/Poras Chaudhary), 8 (Gallo
Images/Salvator Barki), 10 (Image Source), 15 (Taxi Japan/
flashfilm), 16 (Collection: Science Faction/Peter Ginter), 17
(Image Source); Shutterstock pp. 5 (© Lane V. Erickson); 6,
23 bottom (© AXL); 9, 22 top right (© Leungchopan); 11, 22
bottom right, 23 top (© Paul Prescott); 12, 22 bottom left (©
Alexandra Lande); 13 (© Evgeny Murtola); 14, 22 top left (©
Alberto Loyo); 18 (© Emprize); 19 (© Nikos Psychogios); 21
(© Brians); 20, 23 middle (© Dmitry Kalinovsky).

Front cover photograph of a view of New York City, USA,
reproduced with permission of Shutterstock (© MaxyM). Back
cover photograph of a view of a bricklayer reproduced with
permission of Shutterstock (© Dmitry Kalinovsky).

Every effort has been made to contact copyright holders
of any material reproduced in this book. Any omissions will
be rectified in subsequent printings if notice is given to the
publisher.

Contents

What Is a Home?

A home is a place where people live.

Homes keep people safe.

What Is a City?

A city is a place where many people live.

There are cities all over the world.

City Homes

In a city, many people live close to each other.

Some people live in apartments.

Some apartments share courtyards.

balcony

Some apartments have balconies.

Some people live in houses.

row house

Some houses are joined together.

City homes can be different sizes.

Some homes in the middle of a city are small.

Sometimes lots of people live in a small home.

Some homes on the edge of a city are big.

City homes can be different colors.

Some homes are white. They stay cool in hot weather.

What Are City Homes Made Of?

cement

brick

Some homes are made of brick and cement.

Some homes are made from things
other people throw away.

Around the World

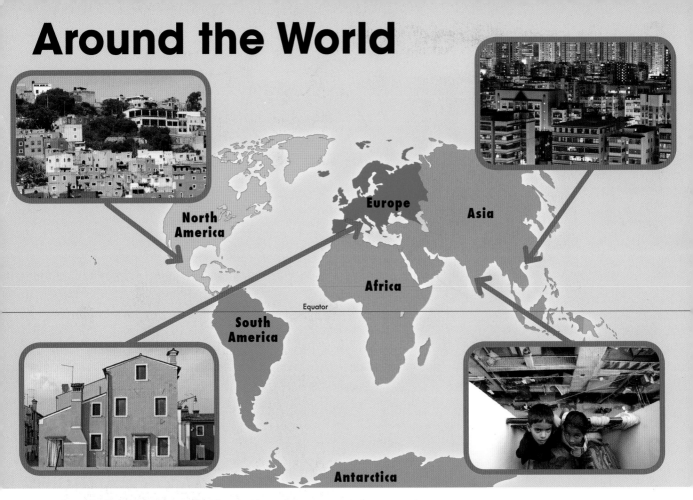

North America

Europe

Asia

Africa

Equator

South America

Antarctica

Follow the arrows to find out where each of these homes are found.

More information on page 24

Picture Glossary

balcony area built out from the wall of a building

cement strong, hard material that can be used to make buildings

city busy place with lots of people, stores, buildings, and roads

Index

Photograph information

The photographs in this book were taken at the following locations: p. 4 United States; p. 6 Barcelona, Spain; p. 7 Delhi, India; p. 8 Istanbul, Turkey; p. 9 Hong Kong; p. 10 Germany; p. 11 Delhi, India; p. 12 Burano, Italy; p. 13 Cambridge, United Kingdom; p. 14 Guanajuato, Mexico; p. 15 Japan; p. 16 Manila, Philippines; p. 17 Quebec, Canada; p. 18 Venice, Italy; p. 19 Amorgos island, Greece; p. 21 Johannesburg, South Africa.

Notes for parents and teachers

Brainstorm different types of homes and encourage children to talk about the homes they live in. Read the book together. Compare the photographs on pages 8 to 9 with the one on page 17. Ask the children why they think homes tend to be close together in a city (lack of space). Show the children pictures of different types of homes for them to identify, or use the images in the book. Include apartments (page 9), a detached house (page 17), a semi-detached house (page 12), and a row house (page 13). Why do they think you can often find blocks of apartments in a city? Look at the homes from around the world and discuss similarities and differences. Explain that we all need homes to keep us safe and protect us from the weather.